For Mom and Dad.
Thanks for helping me build friendships, just by watching yours. —AMS

To Syl —TS

A Note about Mythological Creatures

Except where noted below, the creatures in this story—who are identified at the end of the book—are from Greek mythology.

centaur: half human, half horse, said to behave wildly and show no regard for rules.

Cerberus (Cy's dog): a three-headed dog who watched over the underworld. He stood by the gates letting souls enter, but never letting them leave.

Chelone: a nymph who was turned into a tortoise after she did not make an effort to go to Zeus's wedding.

cyclops (Cy): a giant with one eye in the middle of its forehead. The cyclopes [pl.] were described as strong metalworkers and builders, forging Zeus's thunderbolt, Hades's helmet of invisibility, and Poseidon's trident.

dragon: a winged creature with scales and one or multiple heads. Dragons appear in Greek, Chinese, and other mythologies from all over the world.

Golden Ram: a winged ram with golden fleece. When he died, he was turned into a group of stars called Aries.

hippogriff: created by an Italian poet, it had the head and wings of a Griffin or eagle and the body of a horse. It could fly at incredible speeds.

Hydra: a poisonous water monster with many heads. If one were cut off, another would grow back in its place.

Medusa: a scaled female monster with wings, fangs, claws, and snakes for hair. If anyone looked at her face, they were turned to stone.

Pegasus: a winged horse who entered Mount Olympus and was asked to carry thunderbolts for Zeus.

phoenix (Sunny): a brightly colored, long-lived bird, who after dying in fire was born again from the ashes.

Ratatoskr: a squirrel from Norse mythology who ran up and down the World Tree to carry messages and spread gossip.

Teumessian Fox: a giant fox who was impossible to catch, sent by gods to the city of Thebes as a punishment for the people.

Text copyright © 2017 by Ann Marie Stephens
Illustrations copyright © 2017 by Tracy Subisak
All rights reserved.
For information about permission to reproduce selections from this book, contact permissions@highlights.com.

BOYDS MILLS PRESS
An Imprint of Highlights
815 Church Street
Honesdale, Pennsylvania 18431
Printed in China

ISBN: 978-1-62979-578-2
Library of Congress Control Number: 2016942359

Production by Sue Cole
First edition
The text of this book is set in Typography of coop.
The illustrations were done in pencil and painted digitally.

10 9 8 7 6 5 4 3 2 1

Cy was born to build.

With an eye for detail and the vision to create,

he bends,

molds,

and
THUMP-
THUMP-
THUMPS his hammer
until each masterpiece
is complete.

Cy can make these.

He can make these.

He can even make these.

But he can't make a friend.

Not a real one, anyway.

Making a friend means venturing out.

That can be scary.
So Cy prepares.

He practices polite conversation.

He investigates his dog's flair for friendship.

He tries to look like a friend.

Cy knows it is nice to share.
Maybe he can make something to attract a friend.

He can build a surprise.
Not a seat. Not a box. Not a wagon.

His new friend will ride in a chariot.

But it won't move without wheels.

Being brave takes time.

Cy beams confidence . . . possibly not enough.

He maintains good eye contact . . . perhaps a little too much.

He shows off his wink.

Reconsidering the wink, he heads home.

There Cy raises and rotates until . . .

Hazen Memorial Library
3 Keady Way
Shirley, MA 01464
978.425.2620

... he has a rolling chariot for two.

Cy is one. Who will be two?

At the market, the empty chariot awaits.

Cy beams confidence . . .
just the right amount.

He maintains good eye contact.
Someone else does, too.

Cy's heart **THUMP-THUMP-THUMPS.**

He shares what he has. So does she.

Making a friend
means venturing out.

Pegasus

Medusa

phoenix

Golden Ram

Chelone

Ratatoskr